Dedicated to my parents, Bruce and Lynda McKee.

Dad, thank you for being my "True North" always.

Mom, thank you for providing the most wonderful home growing up in Gonzales, Texas. You taught me to serve the Lord, my family/friends, and my community, including children and adults with speech and language impairments. I am forever grateful.

And, to both of you, for the opportunity to attend the most special place, Texas Christian University. My TCU education gave me skills as a speech language pathologist, the encouragement to write this book, and, most of all, friendships tried and true.

Our faith, our family, and our friends have blessed us beyond belief in this wonderful life.

~Chelle

www.mascotbooks.com

S is the Most Delicious Sound

©2018 Michelle McKee Marlow. All Rights Reserved. No part of this publication may be reproduced, stored in a retrieval system or transmitted in any form by any means electronic, mechanical, or photocopying, recording or otherwise without the permission of the author.

Illustrations by Megan Skeels
Graphic design by Cynthia Wahl

For more information, please contact:
Mascot Books
620 Herndon Parkway #320
Herndon, VA 20170
info@mascotbooks.com

Library of Congress Control Number: 2017960716

CPSIA Code: PRT1217A
ISBN-13: 978-1-68401-777-5

Printed in the United States

S is the Most Delicious Sound

Michelle McKee Marlow

Illustrations by Megan Skeels

Sam can say his Ps and Bs and Vs, but he cannot say the S sound.
And that is a problem, especially today.

Sam wakes up extra early in the morning to practice saying S words. Today is Sam's birthday.

Everyone will want to know how old Sam is. And six is a word that is very hard to say.

Sam's world is full of S sounds.

He lives in Texas, and his sister's name is Susie.

His favorite food is pizza and more than anything else in the world, Sam loves to play baseball.

But whenever Sam tries to say Texas or Susie or baseball or pizza, his tongue gets in the way.

"*Sssss*" sounds like "*thhhhhh.*"
Adults say, "Pardon?" and kids say, "What?"
Sam has to repeat himself over and over.

Every birthday since Sam can remember, he has walked across campus with his mom and sister. They say hello to friends.

They stop for ice cream.

VOLLEYBALL

SPORTS STORE

TCU

TCU

OPEN

BASEBALL

Then they visit the sports store where Sam gets to pick his own birthday present.

This year, Sam wants a brand new baseball, but he is afraid the storeowner won't understand him.

He might have to ask for a volleyball instead.

Sam's mom and sister are all dressed for their walk, but Sam doesn't want to go. "My tongue is too long," Sam says. "I think I should stay home, in my room, in bed."

"Can you touch your tongue to your nose?" Sam's mom asks. Sam tries, but his tongue is too short.

"Can you touch your tongue to your chin?" she asks.
Sam stretches his tongue, but it won't reach that far either.

"Looks like a normal six-year-old tongue to me!" Sam's mom says.
Maybe it's not such a bad day for a walk, Sam decides.

The first person they see on their walk is their neighbor, Mr. Smith. "Hello, Sam. How old are you today?" Mr. Smith asks.

This is the question Sam has been dreading. Sam bites his tongue and holds his breath. Then he gets an idea.

Sam holds up
six fingers.
"Six years old?"
Mr. Smith asks.

Sam nods.
Maybe being six
isn't so terrible
after all.

Next, they stop at Miss Daisy's ice cream stand.
Strawberry ice cream is Sam's favorite, but he is sure
Miss Daisy won't understand him.

"What would you like?" Miss Daisy asks.
Sam hesitates. Then he gets an idea.
He points to the pink ice cream.
"This one?" Miss Daisy asks. "Are you sure?"
Sam nods.

But when Sam tastes his ice cream, he realizes he has made
a mistake.
Yuck, Sam thinks. *This ice cream isn't strawberry—it's sour cherry!*

A few moments later, Sam spots his babysitter, West, walking toward him. By now, sour ice cream is melting down Sam's arm and onto his shoes.

The first thing West says is, "Happy birthday." The second thing he says is, "How old are you now?"

Sam wants to hold up his fingers, but they are all sticky.

Sam panics. He drops his ice cream and runs away as fast as he can.

Sam runs and he runs across the campus commons, down the stairs, and around the corner.

He sits on the edge of Frog Fountain to catch his breath.
Then he hears a sound—*SPLOOSH*—behind him.

"Pssst. Down here," a little voice says.
Sam looks down to find a small, spiky frog staring up at him.

"Hello, I'm SuperFrog," says the frog. "Welcome to my wishing fountain. How can I help you today?"

"But, I didn't make a wish," says Sam. "I do have a problem though," he says next. "My tongue gets in the way and I can't—"

Just then, SuperFrog snaps his tongue in the air and catches a fly.

It is the biggest, longest tongue Sam's eyes have ever seen.

"Deliciousssssss," SuperFrog says, smacking his lips.

It is the most beautiful, crystal clear "*sssss*" Sam's ears have ever heard.

"I wish I could do that," says Sam.

"Eat flies?" asks SuperFrog.

"No," Sam says. "I wish I could make that sound."

"What sound?"

Sam sucks in his breath. He pushes his tongue to his teeth and tries to say "*sssss.*"

But what comes out is a big, wet "*thhhhhh.*"
"Oh, forget it," Sam says, flopping down. "My tongue is too long."

"Unless you're catching flies, the size of your tongue has nothing to do with it," SuperFrog says, hopping closer. "You're not smiling enough. You see, when you frown, your tongue has nowhere to go but out ...

...and down."

SuperFrog frowns and his big, long tongue unfurls across several lily pads.

"But when you hold your head up high and smile," says SuperFrog, "everything works just right. Your tongue rests against your teeth, where nobody sees it. The air slides down your tongue, past your teeth, and out into the world. See?"

SuperFrog's tongue is shaped just like a slide inside his mouth—high at the back and low at the front.

CONFIDENCE

"If you ask me," SuperFrog says, "confidence is the key."

Sam thinks about it for a minute and decides it's true. He *does* frown whenever he says "*sssss*."

"Ahem," says SuperFrog, slapping his foot impatiently.
"If you don't mind—" SuperFrog glances at all the shiny
pennies and nickels and dimes on the fountain floor.
"A frog has to make a living."

"Oh, sorry," Sam says. He pulls a penny from his pocket
and throws it—*SPLOOSH*—into the water.

Then he realizes what he just said—"sorry" with a perfect S.

"Did you hear that, SuperFrog?" Sam asks, but he is suddenly alone. Sam looks all around the fountain. He looks over and under every lily pad. SuperFrog is nowhere to be found.

"But you didn't grant my wish," Sam says to the frog-less fountain.

Just then, Sam's mom comes around the corner.

"For the birthday boy," she says, holding out a brand new ice cream cone.

It even has sprinkles and a cherry on top—and not the sour kind either!

Sam tastes his ice cream—yum, real strawberry—

then he puts a big smile on his face and pushes his tongue

against his teeth.

"Delicioussssth," Sam says.

Susie laughs.

Sam smiles and tries again.

"Delicioussssss," he says
a second time in a
strong, clear voice.

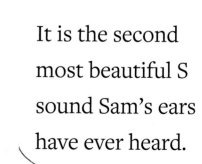

It is the second
most beautiful S
sound Sam's ears
have ever heard.

Sam's sister squeals and claps her hands.

Sam's mom gives him a big birthday hug.

Then they set off for the sports store.

Sam's new baseball is so shiny and fast, he plays catch all day long.

Lots of people stop to ask Sam how old he is.

Sometimes he answers "six" and other times "thicks."
But no matter what comes out of Sam's mouth, he doesn't stop smiling.

After all, it's not every day
he gets to turn six.

For my boys.
Your love and laughter made this possible.

About the Author and Her Table of Six

Michelle bleeds purple! Her passion for TCU shines as she spreads her talent and love around Fort Worth, Texas, as a clinically certified speech language pathologist. She has worked in private practice since 1994, providing services to children, aged birth to high school, with speech and language impairment.

Michelle's biggest passion is her Table of Six: husband Scott Marlow, an anesthesiologist who specializes in cardiac anesthesia, and her four boys, George (19), Thomas (17), Henry (15), and William (10).

Please keep a watchful eye as Michelle and her sister-in-law, Cynthia Marlow, also a clinically certified speech language pathologist, take you on a wonderful journey. They will be publishing books that come with "secret tips" to help tackle speech and language disorders.